Mama Rex and T

The Horrible Play Date

by Rachel Vail

illustrations by Steve Björkman

SCHOLASTIC INC.

New York Toronto London Auckland Sydney
Mexico City New Delhi Hong Kong Buenos Aires

To Jason and Stephen and Hannah
—RV

For Emma Henderson
—SB

No part of this publication may be reproduced in whole or in part,
or stored in a retrieval system, or transmitted in any form
or by any means, electronic, mechanical, photocopying, recording, or otherwise,
without written permission of the publisher.
For information regarding permission, write to Scholastic Inc.,
Attention: Permissions Department, 555 Broadway, New York, NY 10012

ISBN 0-439-28335-3

Text copyright © 2001 by Rachel Vail.
Art copyright © 2001 by Steve Björkman.

All rights reserved. Published by Scholastic Inc.
SCHOLASTIC and associated logos are trademarks and/or
registered trademarks of Scholastic Inc.

12 11 10 9 8 7 6 5 4 3 2 1   1 2 3 4 5 6 7/0

Book design by Chad W. Beckerman

Printed in the U.S.A.
First Scholastic printing, December 2001

Contents

Chapter 1
WAITING

Chapter 2
RAMBUCTIOUS!

Chapter 3
THE CURE

Chapter 1
WAITING

"Where is he?" T asked Mama Rex.

"Relax," said Mama Rex without looking up from the newspaper. "He'll be here soon."

"I can't relax," said T, jumping up beside her. He tried skipping along the couch but he slipped on the Style section and fell onto Mama Rex's lap.

"Oof," said Mama Rex.

"Is it warm enough to go to the playground when he gets here?" T asked.

"I don't know," said Mama Rex. "I can't read the weather report through your head."

T sat up and grabbed Mama Rex by the shoulders. "If it's not, we can play Deep Detective in my room, and my bed could be the bad guys' planet, and we'll throw paint on . . ."

Mama Rex held up her arm.

"Hold on," she said. "I know you're excited because your good friend Walter is coming over. . . ."

"*Best* friend Walter," said T, dancing on the ottoman. "This is going to be the best play date in history!"

T danced so crazily he fell off the ottoman into an upside-down heap on the floor.

"Ouch," said T.

Mama Rex turned T right side up. "This is what happens," she said, "when you act too rambunctious."

"What's rambunctious?" asked T, rubbing the bump on his head.

Mama Rex pulled some newspaper out of T's pajama top. "It means rowdy," she said. "Wild and noisy and out of control."

"We like rambunctious," said T. "The more rambunctious, the better."

The intercom buzzed.

"WALTER!" T yelled.

Mama Rex said, "Please send them up," into the intercom.

"I have to finish my fort!" yelled T, running toward his room.

"Maybe you should put some clothes on first," suggested Mama Rex.

T looked down and noticed what he was wearing. "Oh, yeah."

In his room, T tore off his pajamas, threw them up in the air, and grabbed a bunch of clothes out of his drawers.

He didn't care what he was wearing.

He didn't care if his room was a mess.

He didn't even care that the fort he'd half-made was draped in dirty pajamas.

He only cared that Walter was on his way up in the elevator.

The doorbell rang.

T bounded out of his room, smashed into Mama Rex, grabbed the doorknob, yanked open the door, and shouted, "Walter!"

Walter shouted, "T!"

The play date had begun.

Chapter 2
RAMBUNCTIOUS!

Walter smashed T's fort.

"That's okay," said T. "Wanna play Deep Detective?"

"Bleh," said Walter, and dumped all of T's Legos out of the blue bucket.

"Let's make a truck," suggested T.

"And crash it," said Walter.

"Yeah!" said T. "Unless we really like it."

"Bleh," said Walter. "Smash, crash, blash!"

"Mash!" yelled T.

Walter found some wheels.

T found some axles.

They put them together and the truck was starting to look great.

Walter crashed it into T's bed.

"Walter!" complained T, trying to put it back together.

"Let's play Chinese checkers," said Walter.

"Yeah," said T. "We don't want to be too rambunctious, right?"

"Bleh," said Walter.

Walter crunched over Legos to grab Chinese checkers off the shelf.

Some of the marbles escaped from the box and skittered across the floor.

T grabbed a few. He missed four that rolled under the bed.

"Walter!" yelled T.

"I'm yellow," said Walter.

Yellow was T's favorite color.

Rainbow was Walter's favorite color.

"How about if you're red?" asked T.

"Bleh," said Walter and started setting up the yellow marbles.

T watched him.

T didn't want to be red.

"This is too calm," said T.

"Yeah!" yelled Walter. "Calm is bleh!"

"Yeah!" yelled T. "Let's be rambunctious."

"Yeah!" yelled Walter and threw some marbles into the air.

"Yikes," said T.

Walter was playing soccer and volleyball with the marbles.

"Walter," said T. "Let's start a rock 'n' roll band!"

"Yeah!" yelled Walter, grabbing the drum and a harmonica from T's shelf.

"Yeah!" yelled T. He plugged in his electric guitar and jumped up onto his bed.

Mama Rex stood at the door to T's room, holding her newspaper.

Her mouth was moving but T and Walter could only hear their music.

"Guys?" shouted Mama Rex.

"Ya-doo ya-doo ya-ding dong!" sang Walter.

"We're having fun," explained T.

Mama Rex said some more words. The only one T heard was "calm."

After she left, T stopped playing.

"Do you want to be calm?" he asked Walter.

"No," said Walter, still drumming. "Do you?"

"No," said T. "But maybe something a little tiny bit calmer."

"Let's do an art project!" yelled Walter.

"Yeah!" yelled T.

T took down his art box.

Walter grabbed the good scissors.

T didn't mind because Walter was his best friend.

Walter took the new glue stick and gave T the gunky old one.

T didn't mind because Walter was his best friend.

Walter took the last yellow construction paper and gave T a beige piece.

T didn't mind because Walter was his best friend.

Walter glued the only googly eyeball onto his yellow paper.

T minded a lot.
"That is the last googly eyeball," said T.
"You can use a pom-pom," said Walter.
"A pom-pom?" asked T. "A pom-pom?"
T crumpled his beige paper and threw it.
By accident it hit Walter's ear.

Walter ran screaming to the living room.
T was right behind him.

"I want to go home!" yelled Walter.

"This is the most horrible play date in history," yelled T.

Mama Rex took a sip of her coffee, put her mug on the pile of newspapers on the table, patted the couch on both sides of herself, and asked, "What happened?"

Walter told his side of the story in one breath.

T told his side of the story in one breath.

All Mama Rex heard was, "He took he said scissors pom-pom best only gunky googly glued it chucked it in my eyeball ear!!!!"

Walter and T both sniffled.

"Well," said Mama Rex, standing up. "There's only one thing to do about a gunky gluey only eyeball in your ear."

Walter and T looked at each other out of the corners of their eyes.

They squinched down their eyebrows and shrugged their shoulders.

They had no idea what Mama Rex was talking about.

"Seriously," said Mama Rex. "I read about it in the paper years ago, back when I actually read the paper. There's only one cure for a gunky gluey only eyeball in your ear, otherwise known as a Horrible Play Date."

"What is it?" T asked, quietly.

"Follow me," whispered Mama Rex, heading toward T's room.

Chapter 3
THE CURE

Mama Rex stood at the doorway of T's room.
T and Walter peeked around her.

"It may be difficult to find," said Mama Rex.

"What?" asked Walter.

"The cure for a Horrible Play Date," explained Mama Rex. "It's in here."

"Are you sure?" asked T.

"What does it look like?" asked Walter.

"It's a secret," whispered Mama Rex. "Can you solve the mystery?"

Mama Rex walked away, back to her newspaper and coffee in the living room.

"I have no idea what she's talking about," whispered T.

"She said *it*," said Walter. "That means it's a thing."

"Right," said T. "Good thinking."

They tiptoed into T's room.

They shaded their eyes with their hands.

T and Walter were very experienced at mysteries.

They were Deep Detectives.

"I think I found a clue," said Walter.
He held up a long tubular striped thing.
    "I think you found my pajama bottoms," said T.
    "Oh," said Walter.

"Sometimes clues are hidden under regular junk," said T.

"Good thinking," said Walter. He lifted the drum. Under it was a marble.

"Marbles could be a clue," he said. "Right?"

"Definitely," said T, dumping Legos into the blue bucket.

Wiggling under T's bed to get more marbles, Walter yelled, "I found it!"

"What is it?" T asked.

"I don't know," said Walter. "It's dark under here. And I feel something squishy."

T waited.

Walter wiggled. "I think I'm stuck."

T yanked his friend out from under the bed.

"The cure!" yelled Walter, holding something up in his hand.

T and Walter looked at the thing.

"I think it's fuzz," said T.

"Yeah." Walter sighed. "Fuzz."

"Maybe fuzz is a clue," said T.

Walter smiled. He placed the fuzz on T's dresser, just in case.

T and Walter cleaned and searched and collected.

They got fuzz, marbles, two broken crayons, something that used to be a paper clip, a popped balloon, dirty pajamas, and a googly eyeball.

"Is that the googly eyeball from my art project?" Walter asked.

T shrugged.

"You can have it," whispered Walter.

"That's okay," said T.

"Hey," said Walter. "Maybe we should glue it to your fort."

T and Walter looked around.
The fort was long gone.
"We could build a new fort," suggested T.
"Yeah," said Walter. "And the eyeball could be on the front, watching for clues."
"Yeah!" yelled T.

When Walter's mother came, Walter and T were lying in their new fort, shining flashlights from under blankets onto the googly eyeball.

"We didn't find the cure," mumbled Walter on his way out the door.

"For what?" asked his mother.

"For the Horrible Play Date," said T.

"Yes, you did," said Mama Rex.

Walter turned around. "We did?"

"Was it the fuzz?" asked T.

"No," said Mama Rex. "The cure is just working together."

T and Walter smiled at each other.

"See you tomorrow," said Walter, walking backward and waving good-bye.

T leaned against Mama Rex and waved until Walter was gone.

"I was right," T whispered. "This was the best play date in history."